Summer of Evolution

A Plain Jane Romance Series, Volume 1

P E Murdock

Published by Paul Murdock, 2023.

This is a work of fiction. Similarities to real people, places, or events are entirely coincidental.

SUMMER OF EVOLUTION

First edition. October 20, 2023.

Copyright © 2023 P E Murdock.

ISBN: 979-8223751175

Written by P E Murdock.

To All The Romantic People In The World.

Chapter 1

Jane Smith woke up to the blaring ring of her alarm clock at 6:00 a.m. in her modest one-bedroom apartment. With a groan, she rolled over and slapped the off button, silencing the offensive noise. As Jane slowly sat up, rubbing the sleep from her eyes, she felt the familiar dread settle over her—another day, just like all the ones before it.

Jane, 34, shuffled to the bathroom, lamenting her boring life in Creeksville. She'd lived there her whole life, even going to Creeksville Schools. After earning her teaching degree, she returned to teach near her childhood home.

Jane sighed heavily as she looked at her reflection in the dingy mirror. Her brown hair was a mess, hazel eyes still hazy with sleep. She splashed cold water on her face, dreaming of adventure and escape from monotony.

Shaking her head, Jane brushed aside those fanciful thoughts. She didn't have time for daydreams this morning. It was Monday, which meant getting the kids settled after a weekend at home. Opening the drawer, Jane grabbed her toothbrush and squeezed a line of minty paste onto the bristles. As she brushed, she mentally reviewed her lessons for the week. It was nearing the end of the school year, just three more weeks until summer break. The kids always got antsy this time of year, ready for lazy summer days filled with ice cream and no homework. Jane couldn't blame them. She, too, felt a restlessness in her spirit, a longing for something to break up the repetitive cycle of small-town life.

After rinsing her mouth, Jane returned to her closet and pondered what to wear. Her go-to teaching outfits were comfortable and practical - jeans or slacks paired with a modest blouse or sweater. She selected a pair of faded jeans and a floral print blouse, then added a grey cardigan in case the classroom air conditioning made it chilly. As she changed, Jane couldn't help but envy her best friend Amy and her bold, stylish wardrobe. Amy taught second grade at Cherrywood Elementary and always looked put-together with her trendy outfits and perfect blonde pixie cut. Meanwhile, Jane was stuck in mom jeans and ponytails.

Glancing at the clock, Jane saw it was 6:45 a.m. She hurried to the kitchen and made oatmeal and coffee to go. Her apartment was centrally located, an easy 10-minute drive to Cherrywood, but she liked getting there early to prep. By 7:00 a.m., Jane was out the door, travel mug of coffee in hand.

The roads of Creeksville were quiet this early on a Monday. Jane drove past the quaint downtown, with its locally-owned shops and restaurants already opening for the day. This place truly was stuck in a bygone era, she mused. Turning onto Spruce Street, the lush trees of Creeksville Park came into view, the morning sun glinting off the pond where ducks were already swimming lazily.

Jane pulled into the parking lot of Cherrywood Elementary right at 7:15 a.m. She stepped out of her sedan and took in the familiar sight of the charming brick school building. It looked the same as when she was a student here decades ago, with its big double front doors framed by two small columns. Jane smiled, thinking of all the construction paper hand turkeys and cardboard gingerbread men those doors had seen over the years.

Unlocking her classroom, Jane flicked on the fluorescent lights, illuminating the cheerful space. The walls were painted a bright blue and decorated with colorful alphabet and number posters. Her student's art projects were displayed proudly, their little handprints immortalized in paint. Jane inhaled deeply, taking in the comforting scent of crayons, glue, and construction paper. This room held many memories from her childhood and now new ones with her students.

"Morning, Miss Smith!" called a cheery voice from behind. Jane's teaching assistant, Sandy, was already busy prepping art supplies at one of the kid-sized tables.

"Good morning, Sandy," Jane replied with a smile. Sandy was only a few years older than Jane's students but loved working with children and planned to become a teacher someday. Her peppy demeanor was a nice counterbalance to Jane's more introverted personality.

Jane settled in at her desk and booted up her desktop computer, reviewing the lesson plans for the week. Today, they will be learning about the life cycle of butterflies. Jane had given this lesson every spring for the past seven years since she started kindergarten at Cherrywood: Chrysalis, caterpillar, butterfly. The same four stages are explained similarly: projects assembled from pre-cut shapes. Jane stifled a yawn. Would it be so bad to try something different for once?

The morning bell rang at 8:00 a.m. sharp, jolting Jane from her thoughts. Her students began filtering in, their sneakers squeaking on the polished floor. They chatted animatedly about their weekends as they hung up backpacks and lunch boxes. Jane felt her earlier melancholy fade away as she was swept up in the enthusiasm and energy of her kids. Their faces lit up when they saw the art supplies laid out.

"Today we're going to learn about the magical transformation butterflies go through called metamorphosis," Jane began, holding up a picture book titled From Egg to Butterfly. The lesson proceeded smoothly; the students were ooh-ing and aah-ing over the illustrations. Jane found herself getting caught up in their awe and seeing the life cycle with new eyes, as if for the first time. They then set to work decorating their paper butterfly puppets. The classroom was filled with the sounds of giggling, scissors snipping, and glue sticks squeezing out sticky strands.

Before Jane knew it, the lunch bell rang at 11:30 a.m. The kids eagerly lined up, and she walked them down to the cafeteria, reminding them to use inside voices. She then headed to the teacher's lounge to meet Amy for their daily lunch date.

The teacher's lounge was painted an inoffensive beige and smelled perpetually of burned coffee. A couple of round tables were tucked in the corner by the kitchenette, and worn tweed sofas lined the walls. Jane grabbed a prepackaged salad from the fridge and joined Amy at their regular table.

"So, how's Monday treating you so far?" Amy asked, popping a grape tomato into her mouth. Her bubbly personality contrasted with the dull decor.

"Oh, you know, same old," Jane replied with a shrug, spearing some limp lettuce leaves. She described her butterfly lesson for the millionth time, unable to mask the boredom in her voice.

Amy nodded sympathetically. "I feel you. The end of the year is rough. But just hang in there, summer will be here before you know it!"

Jane sighed. "I guess you're right. It's just hard to get excited about summer vacation when every summer has been exactly the same. Living in this little town, it's like I'm stuck in a time loop."

"Girl, you need an adventure!" Amy exclaimed. "A chance to get out there and shake things up. You should plan a fun trip this summer, something totally out of your comfort zone."

Jane's eyes lit up at the thought. A trip somewhere far from Creeksville, somewhere wild and exotic and thrilling. She imagined white water rafting through raging rapids or hiking mist-shrouded mountains far from civilization. It was just the escape she craved from her repetitive life.

"You know what?" Jane said slowly. "I think I will plan a trip. Something to really challenge myself."

Amy beamed. "Atta girl! I'm here to help. Let's find the perfect adventure for you.

The lunch bell rang, signaling the end of their break. Jane waved goodbye to Amy and returned to her classroom, excited to have something to look forward to. A chance to finally shake things up and add some color to the mundane gray haze her life had become.

The rest of the week, she passed in a blur of finger painting, show-and-tell, and ABA song singalongs. By the time Friday afternoon rolled around, Jane's anticipation had built to a fever pitch. She bounced on her heels as she waited for the dismissal bell, ready to start planning her trip. At 3:00 p.m. sharp, the piercing ring sounded, and her students stampeded for the door in a flurry of backpack straps and light-up sneakers.

Jane tidied up the classroom, dumping out bins of torn construction paper scraps and wiping down glue-crusted tables. Her mind kept wandering as she imagined all the possibilities for her upcoming adventure. A week lounging on tropical beaches in the Caribbean? No, it's too dull and predictable. Backpacking across Europe? I need to be more adventurous. Jane wanted something rugged and remote, totally divorced from her mundane reality.

As she flipped off the light switch, her eyes lit up. She would go camping—no, backpacking!—in a remote wilderness area, totally alone. Jane had never camped a day but was determined to challenge herself. Her next step with the location narrowed down would be planning the logistics. Feeling energized, Jane hurried out to her car, ready to get started.

That evening, Jane sat curled up on her lumpy futon, laptop glowing before her. She had changed into cozy pajamas and pulled her hair into a messy topknot. Her cat, Mars, a fluffy ginger tabby, was curled beside her, purring softly.

"What do you think, Mars? The Grand Canyon? Yellowstone? Alaska?" Jane mused as she scrolled through photos of breathtaking parks and forests. She wanted somewhere rugged, off the beaten path. Somewhere that would push her limits.

Mars yawned, kneading his paws into the quilt. He did not grasp the gravity of this major life decision.

After hours of searching, Jane finally settled on the perfect location: the remote Gila National Forest in New Mexico. Known for its soaring mountains, deep canyons, and dense forests, it was a landscape far different from the rolling hills surrounding Creeksville. She could enter its 5,000 square miles of wilderness for an authentic backcountry experience.

Next came the matter of supplies. Having never camped before, Jane needed gear and help figuring out where to start. She made a checklist for a week-long backcountry trip: tent, sleeping bag, cooking gear, first aid kit, freeze-dried food—lots of shopping to do.

Jane spent the weekend dragging a bemused Amy around massive sporting goods stores, gathering all her supplies. Amy helped her select a sturdy but lightweight one-person tent. She showed her the difference between a mummy and a rectangular sleeping bag. They debated the merits of different hiking boots and backpack styles. By Sunday evening, Jane had neatly piled everything in her living room. She stood back to admire the mound of outdoor gear, feeling both proud and terrified. This was happening.

The school week crawled by at a snail's pace. Jane could barely focus, instead doodling campfire sketches and s'mores in the margins of her lesson plan book. Her students' excitement for summer break now matched her own. On Friday, Jane handed out the final report cards. She hugged teary-eyed kids goodbye, wishing them a fun and safe vacation.

On the last day of the workweek, Jane and Amy went out for a celebratory happy hour cocktail to commemorate the start of summer...and Jane's impending adventure. They sat at a tall table at Creeksville's one hipster-ish bar, an exposed-brick joint called The Drunken Monk.

"I can't believe you're actually doing this," Amy said, toying with the citrus wedge on her glass. "My little Jane, all grown up and going on a wilderness backpacking trip!"

Jane smiled. "I know, it's crazy! I'm terrified but also so ready for something different." She took a sip of her grapefruit vodka spritzer. "Hopefully, I don't get eaten by a bear," she said nervously.

"You're going to do amazing," Amy said supportively. "Just promise you'll call me if you need absolutely anything. And I expect a full report when you're back!"

"Deal!" Jane said, lifting her glass to clink Amy's. She was lucky to have such an amazing best friend.

Jane loaded her sedan with all her brand-new camping gear the following day. She triple-checked that she had the lengthy list of supplies, then locked up her apartment. Sliding behind the wheel, she took a deep breath. This was it.

"Look out, Gila National Forest. Here I come!" Jane said aloud. With excitement and trepidation, she pulled out of the parking lot. She headed towards the highway that would take her out of Creeksville. After 34 uneventful years in this sleepy town, her first real adventure was about to begin.

Chapter 2

Today was the day she would finally embark on her solo camping trip into the remote wilderness of the Gila National Forest. As much as the idea thrilled her, she couldn't ignore the butterflies swarming in her stomach.

Sitting in bed, Jane glanced around her modest one-bedroom apartment, taking in the familiar surroundings. She would miss the cozy comfort of home while roughing it in the woods, but she needed this adventure to break free from the mundane routine of small-town life.

Jane slid out from under her quilt and padded to the bathroom, stifling a yawn. She smiled softly at the sight of Mars, her ginger tabby cat, curled up asleep on the bath mat. At least he would be safe and content staying with Amy while Jane was away.

After brushing her teeth and splashing cold water on her face to wake up, Jane shuffled to the kitchen to make coffee. The rich aroma soon filled the small space as the pot brewed. Jane poured herself a steaming mug and added a splash of cream, savoring the comforting warmth in her hands.

Leaning against the counter, Jane looked around at the granite counters and honey oak cabinets she had picked out when she bought the place after college. It wasn't glamorous, but she was proud to own her first home. She would miss the little place while out in the untamed wilderness. At least Amy promised to water her plants and collect the mail.

It was nearly 6 a.m. Jane took a deep breath and opened the closet. She pondered her options, wanting comfortable clothes for the long drive ahead. Jane selected a pair of worn jeans, hiking boots, and a green flannel shirt. She braided back her wavy brown hair to keep it out of her face for the drive.

After drinking a protein bar and banana for breakfast, Jane checked the extensive camping supply list she had meticulously prepared. She wanted to be ready for any situation in the remote forest. The tent, sleeping bag, first aid kit, and freeze-dried food were accounted for.

Jane quickly thanked Amy for taking care of the apartment and Mars. She promised to call as soon as she was back from the trip. Jane knew she was lucky to have such an amazing best friend.

At precisely 7:00 a.m., Jane lugged the heavy bags and supplies she had packed the night before down to her sedan. She had to push hard to make everything fit in the trunk and backseat. After locking up, Jane slid into the driver's seat, keys in hand. This was it - time for the adventure she had been dreaming of.

Jane cruised through the empty streets of downtown Clarksville, smiling fondly at the quaint locally-owned shops and restaurants. Though she was eager to escape the repetitive rhythm of small-town life for a while, she did love her cozy hometown.

As Jane drove past the lush park and sparkling pond at the edge of town, she felt a swell of excitement building inside her. Tomorrow, she would set up camp in the rugged Gila wilderness, far from the world she knew. She turned up the radio and sang along, ready for the open road.

The highway stretched on for miles and miles, framed by rolling green hills dotted with grazing cattle. Jane smiled, enjoying the drive and freedom of being alone. She once stopped at a rest stop to stretch her legs and use the bathroom. The reality of what she was doing - willingly traveling alone into the unknown - began to sink in.

As the terrain gradually grew more mountainous and the forests thicker, Jane knew she must be getting close. She had never ventured anywhere near this remote corner of New Mexico. Jane's hands gripped the wheel tighter as the paved road turned gravel. There were no signs of civilization now, only hills densely blanketed in towering Ponderosa pines.

When Jane crossed a wooden bridge over a rushing river, she decided to stop and consult the park map. According to the guide, she should be nearing the Canyon Trailhead, where she planned to begin her backpacking journey. Jane smoothed out the crinkled map, tracing her route along the winding trails with one finger.

Glancing at her watch, she saw it was just past noon. Jane's stomach growled loudly in the quiet car. She rummaged in her pack and found an apple and peanut butter crackers to curb her hunger. Jane studied the map as she ate, trying to imprint every detail. She didn't want to get lost out here alone.

After a quick bathroom break in the bushes, Jane laced up her hiking boots and sprayed herself with bug spray. After the long drive, she did a few lunges and squats to warm up her muscles. Slinging her heavy backpack over her shoulders, Jane took a steadying breath. She had memorized the first miles of the trail and knew to follow the river north.

"Here goes nothing," Jane said aloud, peering into the dark forest ahead. She glanced back at her car one last time, then stepped onto the trail. The gravel crunched under her boots with each stride. Jane inhaled the crisp pine-scented air, scanning the scenery in wonder. She was doing this!

The Canyon Trail was initially relatively flat, following the riverbank beneath a thick canopy of trees. Sunlight filtered through the branches in patches. Jane smiled as a squirrel scolded her from a nearby oak, its furry body twitching indignantly. She took her time, wanting to take advantage of this memorable experience.

After about two miles, the trail climbed in elevation as it veered away from the river and deeper into the forested hills. Jane welcomed the burn in her legs. She focused on her breath, finding a steady hiking rhythm. The physical exertion helped settle her nerves.

Jane was amazed by the diversity of trees towering above her - stately firs, scrubby junipers, and, of course, the towering Ponderosas, New Mexico's iconic pine. She trailed her hand along their deeply furrowed bark as she walked. Jane wondered how old these wise giants were. Centuries, probably.

The afternoon wore on, the shadows growing longer as the sun sank lower on the horizon. Jane stopped occasionally to sip some water and have a quick snack to keep her energy up. As the trail continued to climb, she was thankful for the hiking poles she had borrowed from Amy for balance.

When Jane rounded a switchback, and the land dropped away, an incredible vista opened up. She gasped aloud, taking in the sweeping view. Unending ridges folded into the distance, blanketed in pines, dotted with crimson manzanita bushes. Far below, the river shone like a silver ribbon.

Jane quickly snapped some photos with her phone to show Amy later. As beautiful as the landscape photos online had been, they paled compared to seeing the real thing in all its wild glory. She stood utterly transfixed, feeling like the only person in the world.

Finally tearing her eyes away, Jane continued along the trail as it leveled out on the ridgeline. She decided to start scouting for a campsite even though only a few hours of daylight left. Jane wanted ample time to gather firewood and set up her new gear.

She passed a few suitable spots, but they needed to be more appropriate. Too rocky, too slanted, too close to the trail. After another half mile, she spotted a nearly perfect site tucked under the boughs of a towering Ponderosa. The tree's sprawling roots offered a sheltered nook, and the ground was flat and soft with pine needles.

Jane eagerly slipped off her pack and stretched her weary shoulders. She took a long sip of water and built a fire ring to contain the flames. Jane grunted as she rolled some heavy rocks into place, forming a circle. Amy was right - she needed to hit the gym more.

Next, Jane unfurled her brand-new tent and stared at the poles and clips with confusion. She had forgotten to practice setting it up before the trip. After several failed attempts, Jane collapsed on the ground laughing. If only her students could see her now!

With patience and many deep breaths, Jane finally constructed a passable dome shelter. She smoothed out the rain fly and secured it with the provided stakes and cords. Jane beamed proudly and went inside her tiny nylon home to lay out her sleeping pad and bag. Cozy!

Now for the fire. Jane gathered an armful of dry pine needles, twigs, and strips of bark. She arranged them carefully in the stone ring and lit a match. The fuel immediately crackled to life, flames licking upward. Jane pumped her fist and did a victory dance at successfully starting her first campfire.

As dusk fell over the silent forest, Jane heated a packet of dehydrated stroganoff on the fire. She added some rehydrating dried veggies to round out the meal. It wasn't gourmet, but Jane didn't care. Feeling utterly content, she ate under the stars at the rough-hewn picnic table.

With her belly full and body weary from the long hike, Jane was ready to curl up in her tent. She cleaned up her cooking gear using minimal water, not wanting to attract bears. After hanging her food bag from a high branch, Jane climbed into her cozy sleeping bag as darkness descended. The crackling fire and forest sounds soon lulled her to sleep.

Jane awoke with the first light filtering through the nylon tent walls. She emerged, stretching, and took in the stunning view of the river valley below bathed in dawn's rosy glow. After visiting the camp bathroom area, Jane boiled water on her stove to make instant coffee.

Jane sipped the hot coffee on a log by the smoldering fire ring. She watched the rising sun slowly illuminate the forest. She breathed deeply, feeling genuinely relaxed for the first time in ages. The fresh, earthy smells of pine needles and rich soil filled her nose. Jane smiled, thinking she could get used to this.

Jane efficiently packed her minimal gear after breakfast, oatmeal, and dried fruit. She buried the fire ashes with dirt to thoroughly extinguish any lingering embers before hitting the trail again. Her body was pleasantly sore, but she looked forward to a full day of hiking ahead.

Jane planned to follow Canyon Trail until it connected with the Gila River Trail. According to the guidebook, that path led to all sorts of natural wonders - waterfalls, hot springs, ancient cliff dwellings. Excitement bubbled in Jane's chest as she walked, thrilled to explore it all.

The morning passed enjoyably as Jane steadily walked deeper into the backcountry. The landscape grew more rugged and untamed. Jane often paused to examine unique plants and flowers up close. She spotted a family of coatis scrounging under some bushes; their long striped tails held upright.

When she heard the distant roar of falling water, Jane hurried. Rounding a curve, she caught her first glimpse of Whitewater Falls. Jane's jaw dropped at the sight. The mighty cascade plummeted over a sheer cliff, crashing into the rocks below and sending a fine mist.

Jane edged as close as she safely could, mesmerized by the raw, primal force of the massive waterfall. She closed her eyes and inhaled the clean mineral scent of the pounding water. Jane knew at that moment she had made the right choice coming here alone. This beauty was worth any struggle.

Pulling herself away from the falls, Jane continued down the trail, keeping her eyes peeled for the promised hot springs. Jane squealed with delight when she smelled the sulfurous odor and saw rising steam. She all but ran the last stretch of trail to the springs.

Finding a secluded pool, Jane quickly stripped down to her swimsuit underneath. She sank into the deliciously hot, bubbling water, instantly soothed. As Jane closed her eyes and leaned back to wet her hair, she silently thanked the universe for guiding her here.

After her soak, Jane reluctantly dragged herself out and got dressed again. The sun was sinking fast, so she focused on hiking a couple of miles left to the designated backcountry campground. Other backpackers would be staying there, but Jane didn't mind. She looked forward to cooking dinner over a natural shared fire pit.

Jane arrived just before dusk, relieved to take her pack off. She saw a few other small tents already set up nearby. The campers gathered around the roaring fire, welcomed Jane, and offered her a seat on one of the provided logs. Jane smiled shyly but accepted, eager to chat after two days alone.

One kind older man named Walt shared his camp chair with Jane and offered her a burger from the grill they had set up. She devoured it hungrily. As the flickering fire lit their faces, the group traded stories late into the night about their wilderness adventures so far. Jane felt suddenly grateful, realizing this solo journey had connected her with humanity and nature in a profound new way. She tucked happily into her sleeping bag, feeling blessed.

The next several days passed in a blissful blur as Jane sank deeper into the rhythms of forest life. She would wake up with the sun each morning, brew coffee on the camp stove, and greet her new friends. After breakfast, she'd pack a small day pack and hit the trail, sometimes alone, sometimes joining others.

Jane was continuously amazed by the diversity of the landscape within the sprawling park's borders. One day, she hiked through grassy meadows ablaze with wildflowers, stopping often to photograph the vibrant colors. The next, she trekked miles through steep switchbacks, ascending exposed cliffs with dizzying drops. Every turn revealed new beauty.

In the afternoons, Jane would return to the camp dusty and tired but excitedly over her latest discoveries. She learned to build the perfect fire and happily helped prepare communal meals with the ingredients everyone contributed. At night, glowing in the firelight, the conversation and laughter flowed freely between old friends and new.

Jane took a long, peaceful hike along the Gila River on her final day. She found a sunny, flat boulder and reclined on its warm surface. Jane took out her journal and pen, reflecting on everything she had experienced in the past week alone in the wilderness. She wrote about her sense of wonder at nature's magic and power. Jane reflected on her journey, feeling more capable and alive than ever. As the sun set, she returned to camp for dinner with her friends. They toasted the beauty of the Gila and promised to meet again here someday. After heartfelt goodbyes, Jane retired to her tent and snuggled deep into her cozy sleeping bag. She would hike out tomorrow and begin the long drive back home, but she knew part of her spirit would always remain in this sacred wilderness. She drifted off with a contented smile on her face, changed forever.

Jane awoke at 5 a.m. to the melodic call of a canyon wren outside her tent. She dressed quickly in the pre-dawn stillness, then headed to the camp kitchen to prepare breakfast. Jane smiled fondly at the cold fire ring, remembering the warmth and laughter it had hosted over the past week. After cleaning up, she hoisted her heavy pack. She looked around the camp, saying goodbye to this place that now held so many memories.

The hike out was bittersweet, but Jane's heart swelled with gratitude for all she had experienced here. The solitude in nature had recharged her spirit and shown her just how resilient she could be. Jane knew she would return home re-energized and open to whatever life brought next.

As Jane followed the winding trail back down to the trailhead parking lot, she paused often to soak up the tranquil beauty around her one last time. She breathed deeply of the crisp pine-scented air and trailed her fingers over the deeply furrowed bark of the trees as she passed.

When the parking area finally appeared, Jane quickened her tired steps, suddenly eager to share all her stories with Amy. She knew her best friend would be thrilled to hear how much Jane had embraced this journey of self-discovery.

Unlocking her dusty sedan, Jane collapsed into the driver's seat with a grateful sigh. She took a long swig of cool water and dug into her pack for the bags of trail mix to snack on during the drive home. Jane turned the key in the ignition, bid one final farewell to the soaring forest ridges, and pulled onto the gravel road leading back to civilization, feeling blissful and free.

Chapter 3

J ane slowly opened her eyes, momentarily confused by her surroundings. Then it all came flooding back - the 13-hour drive from San Francisco, arriving at Willow Creek National Park late last night, attempting to set up her new tent by headlamp. This was the start of Jane's spontaneous solo camping trip, a week in the wilderness to clear her head after her terrible breakup with David.

As morning light filtered through the nylon walls, Jane sat up and stretched, her whole body stiff and achy from a night on the hard ground. She had tossed and turned all night on her flimsy sleeping pad, kept awake by noises of snapping twigs and rustling bushes. Every sound made her heart race, convinced a bear or wildcat was lurking right outside.

Jane fumbled with the tent zipper and crawled outside, shivering as the cool morning air hit her skin. The trees surrounding the campsite were bathed in an ethereal golden light, and a low mist clung to the ground. Jane walked to the shared campground bathroom facility to brush her teeth and change into hiking clothes. When she emerged, feeling slightly more human, she saw an older couple at the site beside hers, already brewing coffee over a crackling fire. Jane envied their well-worn camp chairs and fully stocked cooler as she eyed her mess of supplies spilling haphazardly from her car.

Heading back to her site, Jane knew her first order of business was making coffee. She needed caffeine before tackling any other camp tasks. Rummaging through her food tub, Jane found the instant coffee and stainless steel percolator she had bought just for this trip. Jane arranged some twigs and pinecones on the fire ring, mimicking what she had seen the neighbors do. She lit a match and held it to the kindling. It flared briefly, then fizzled out, leaving only wisps of white smoke. Jane coughed as the smoke wafted into her face. Okay, take two. She lit another match and tried again. Still no fire, more smoke stinging her eyes.

After several more failed attempts, Jane was out of matches. The kind older man next door noticed her struggling and wandered over.

"Having some trouble getting that campfire going?" he asked. His voice was friendly, not condescending.

Jane smiled sheepishly. "Is it that obvious?"

The man chuckled. "Here, let me give you a few pointers."

He showed Jane how to gather dry, fluffy fuel first and then add slightly larger kindling over it and demonstrated building a tepee shape with the logs. As he talked, Jane realized she should have paid more attention to fire-building instead of fantasizing about s'mores when she watched YouTube videos about camping.

"The wood out here is still a bit damp from the rain last week, so you have to be extra careful with your tinder so it catches quick," he explained.

When he struck a match this time, the fuel blazed immediately. Jane let out a yelp of delight as she watched the flames spread to the kindling and logs.

"Thank you so much! I'm pretty new to this," Jane admitted.

"No problem at all. Happy to help. My name's Walt, and that's my wife Ruth over there." He gestured to the petite, white-haired woman reading in one of the camp chairs.

"I'm Jane. Thanks for saving me from my incompetence," Jane replied with an appreciative smile. After exchanging a few more pleasantries, Walt strolled back to his site, leaving Jane alone with her newfound fire.

She triumphantly hung her percolator over the flames and soon had hot, delicious coffee brewing. Sipping the steaming mug, Jane plopped in one of her cheap folding camp chairs. Looking around the site, she felt her spirits sink. Her tent was pitched haphazardly, with one side drooping perilously low to the ground. Her clothes and food were strewn around chaotically. She had somehow bent one of her telescoping roasting sticks trying to assemble it last night. Walt and Ruth's site looked out of a camping magazine, with everything neatly in its place. Jane pictured David's contemptuous expression if he could see her bumbling around out here in the wilderness.

She quickly banished the thought of her ex. This trip was about focusing on herself, not the past. David constantly criticized Jane's outdoor incompetence, finding her childlike awe of nature absurd. "It's just trees and dirt, babe. I don't get why you're so fascinated by it," he had scoffed once when she stopped to admire a sunset on a hike. His condescension was just one of their many incompatibilities. Well, now Jane could bask in as many golden sunsets as she wanted without judgment.

After finishing her coffee, Jane decided to try setting up her tent correctly in the light of day. She read the instructions three times, laying each pole and rod in order. When she started connecting the pieces, they seemed to have a mind of their own, bending and twisting out of her grasp. Jane wrestled with the uncooperative poles, threading them through the tent fabric. As she connected the final pole, the entire structure collapsed loudly. Jane yelped as the tent folded, trapping her half inside. She flailed around, finally freeing herself and emerging with pine needles clinging to her hair.

"Everything okay over there?" Walt called out.

Jane flushed with embarrassment. "Just struggling with this tent a bit," she replied, her voice muffled by nylon.

"Need a hand?" Walt stood up from his camp chair, looking concerned yet amused.

"No, thank you though," Jane answered hurriedly. She was mortified at her tent incompetence being on full display. "I'll figure it out," she said with more confidence than she felt.

Walt just nodded and sat back down. After two more cringe-worthy tent failures, Jane had finally erected it in a somewhat stable manner. The bottom edges didn't look quite taut enough, and she was sure the rainfly was inside out. But it would suffice for now. Exhausted, Jane slumped back into her camp chair. Then she remembered she should probably eat breakfast at some point.

Reluctantly, she shuffled over to her haphazard pile of food. Instant oatmeal seemed the most straightforward meal she could manage. Ripping open a packet, she suddenly realized she had no clean utensils or bowls. Jane glanced sheepishly at Walt and Ruth's well-stocked camp kitchen, then back at her lack of anything. Sighing, she ate the dry oatmeal straight from the packet, washing it with more coffee. Later, she made a mental note to buy bowls and cutlery at the camp store. And pick up a camping cookbook while she was there.

The morning passed quickly as Jane tried to organize her gear and make her site feel cozier. She strung up twinkly white lights along the tent roof - they lent a magical charm against the dull beige nylon. Jane unpacked her camping lounge chair, cushier than the basic one she brought for the first night. She floated the idea of a DIY fire pit circle when a parked truck approached the site entrance. A tall, muscular man stepped out wearing a park ranger's signature gray and green uniform. Early-to-mid-40s, chiseled jawline with stubble. He lifted his ranger hat to reveal a head of thick, wavy dark hair peppered with gray at the temples. Despite looking like he had stepped right off the pages of an LL Bean catalog, his demeanor was warm and unassuming.

"Morning folks, just coming through to check permits," he called out, strolling over to Walt and Ruth's site first and seeing the ranger reminded Jane that she had been so eager to get on the road yesterday that she had forgotten to display her permit. She frantically tore through her glovebox until she located the printed permit and stumbled over to stake it into the ground as the ranger approached.

"Cutting it a bit close there," he said good-naturedly, reading over the permit to confirm her checkout date.

"Sorry, I was just so excited to get here yesterday I forgot what mattered," Jane admitted.

The ranger smiled, his slate gray eyes crinkling at the corners. "Happens all the time. What matters is that you're out here now enjoying this place. I'm Mark, one of the park rangers here."

"I'm Jane. And yeah, it's so beautiful, I almost can't believe it's real," Jane said enthusiastically, gazing up at the soaring pines.

Mark followed her gaze. "It's quite something. I've been working here for over a decade, and it still takes my breath away." "Wow, that must be an amazing job." Do you get to explore the park a lot?"

"I do—scouting trails, monitoring wildlife, rescuing the occasional lost hiker," Mark replied with a chuckle. His deep laugh made Jane instantly want to join in. "I'm actually headed out soon to check out potential storm damage on some of the trails."

Jane perked up at this. "Storm damage, huh? That sounds exciting."

She didn't know what made her continue. Maybe the romance of the wilderness was getting to her already. "Any chance I could tag along? I'd love to see more of the park with someone who really knows the area."

Mark looked hesitant like he was trying to formulate a polite rejection. But then he seemed to reconsider. You could join for a bit. I'm heading to Burned Oak Trail. It's one of the more challenging in the park, though."

"That's perfect! I need a challenge," Jane exclaimed. In reality, the most strenuous hiking she had done recently was trekking up the paved paths in Golden Gate Park. But she wasn't going to admit that now.

"Alright then. Meet me back here at the truck in 15 minutes," Mark instructed. "Make sure to wear sturdy hiking boots and bring plenty of water."

Jane could barely contain her excitement. "You got it!"

Jane marveled at her audacity as she hurried to prepare, inviting herself to Mark's work expedition. She could imagine what David or her other play-it-safe exes would think. But for once, Jane didn't care.

She had come here to get out of her comfort zone, have adventures, and embrace life. Tagging along with a handsome park ranger seemed like a thrilling way to start.

Fifteen minutes later, Jane was waiting eagerly by the truck, wearing her new hiking boots and athleisure clothes from REI that now felt like an embarrassing costume. Mark strode up looking like the Marlboro man incarnate, complete with a worn leather rucksack dangling from his broad frame. Jane smiled and waved, trying not to seem overeager.

"Glad you could make it," Mark said, holding the truck's passenger door open. "The trailhead is just a few miles up."

Jane climbed in, tingling with excitement and a bit of nerves. What would their small talk even consist of? Would he ask about her camping experience and see right through her outdoorsy facade? She decided to start by peppering him with questions—people always liked talking about themselves.

"So how long have you been a ranger here?" Jane asked as they bumped up the gravel road away from the campground.

"Let's see, about 12 years now," Mark replied, keeping his eyes on the road. "I worked in banking before that, if you can believe it. But I got sick of the office, the suits and ties. After my divorce, I just wanted to get as far away from that life as possible. A buddy suggested I look into the park service, and here I am."

"Wow," Jane said, surprised at how open he was already. "That's quite the career change. Banker to the mountain man."

Mark chuckled. "It's been a good switch. Hard to beat spending every day out in nature."

"It really is gorgeous here," Jane agreed, gazing out at the forest flowing past her window. "Do you ever miss parts of regular life, though? Movies, restaurants, Target runs?"

"Sometimes, I guess." Mark kept his eyes on the road. "But the solitude out here suits me well. More of a hermit these days, by choice."

Jane sensed she had surfaced on a sensitive topic and decided to shift gears. "So tell me about Burned Oak Trail. How'd it get that name?"

Mark seemed to relax again as he gave her an overview of the trail, deep in the heart of an old fire-scarred forest. He pointed out charred tree trunks as they arrived at the trailhead. Taking a final swig of water, Jane hopped out of the truck, trying to look athletic.

"Ready for your first burn hike?" Mark asked, handing Jane a topo trail map from his pack.

"Let's do this!" Jane said with forced enthusiasm. In reality, the steep, winding trail looked daunting, swallowed up by the forest ahead of them. She jammed the map in her pocket and hoped she wouldn't need it.

They set off together down the trail, Mark matching his pace to Jane's. The path started relatively smooth before quickly narrowing and winding steeply up a ridge. Rocky switchbacks and exposed roots required careful foot placement. Mossy fallen logs obstructed their path periodically. Jane was already short of breath and sweating in an unattractive way. She focused on putting one foot before the other and tried not to seem outwardly pathetic.

"It's a leg burner but worth it for the views up top," Mark encouraged, barely sounding winded. He pointed out interesting plants and rock formations, explaining their geological histories as they walked. Jane asked question after question, partly because she was genuinely interested but mostly so she wouldn't have to talk about herself. Mark seemed more than happy to indulge her curiosity. He was passionate about the park and enjoyed sharing his knowledge.

They continued trekking up the trail, sometimes single file, across flower-strewn meadows and gurgling streams on mossy logs. Jane was enthralled by the park's raw, wild beauty even as her legs started to shake and her socks bunched uncomfortably. After a particularly rocky scramble up a section ironically called Ladder Hill, Mark paused to wait for Jane, who was now straggling far behind, sweaty and panting.

"Why don't we take a quick break?" he suggested kindly when Jane finally crested the hill, looking half-dead. She gratefully slumped onto a fallen log, guzzling water. Mark sat beside her on the log, barely phased by the strenuous hiking. His muscular thighs rippled through his cargo pants.

Jane tried not to stare. Fumbling for a topic, she gestured vaguely at the surrounding meadow. "Um, lovely flowers!"

"Indeed! These are called Parnassia, or grass of Parnassus," Mark said, admiring the delicate white blooms swaying in the breeze. "I love how they almost glow against the dark burnt trees."

Jane followed his gaze up to the soaring blackened trunks around them, carved with spiral patterns from the long-ago flames. "It's kind of eerie, but beautiful too, in a melancholy way. Everything the fire destroyed, and yet the forest is still alive," she mused.

Mark nodded thoughtfully. "I couldn't have put it better myself. You have a poet's soul."

Jane blushed, taken aback by the compliment after her long string of dumb "nature is pretty" comments. They sat without speaking momentarily, letting the gentle breeze work its calm magic. Jane could almost feel her stress and sadness about David sloughing off, carried away by the wind through the scorched pines.

When Jane had caught her breath, they pressed on up the trail, which was mercifully smoother for a while. Cresting a hill, Mark paused dramatically. "Ladies and gentlemen, the main attraction." He swept his arm out with a flourish. Jane gasped as they emerged from the forest into a rocky clearing with panoramic views. The valley fell away beneath them, a river winding through like a glistening blue ribbon. Snow-capped peaks loomed in the distance.

"Wow," Jane breathed. "This is... I don't even have words."

"Right?" Mark grinned. "I never get tired of this view. On a clear day you can even see all the way to the Sierras."

Jane tried to memorize every detail to hold back home in her boxlike apartment. A lucky breeze blew, cooling her sweat-dampened brow. She had come for this—a total immersion in nature's glory, far from the city bustle. Jane wished she could build a little cabin right here and stay forever.

They ate a quick snack and then started back down the trail. The descent proved almost more burdensome on Jane's legs than the ascent. Loose gravel shifted dangerously under her boots. She fell behind Mark again, envying his graceful, agile strides. He found the most solid spots to land each step intuitively. Jane was grateful when Mark didn't seem impatient at her slow pace.

Rounding a wooded switchback, Jane lost her footing on a sneaky tree root and started careening sideways off the trail. She flailed her arms to regain balance, but her momentum carried her fast toward a sharp drop-off. Jane squeezed her eyes shut, bracing for impact with the unforgiving ground.

Suddenly, a firm hand grasped her arm in an iron grip, yanking Jane forcefully back onto the trail. She collapsed against a sturdy chest just as she started to topple over the ledge. Jane looked up into Mark's slate gray eyes, now dark with worry. His arms were still wrapped tightly around her, their bodies pressed together.

"You alright? That was a close one," Mark said gruffly.

Jane's tongue felt thick in her mouth. All she could do was nod mutely as adrenaline coursed through her veins.

Chapter 4

The first rays of sunlight filtered through the nylon walls of her tent. She lay still for a moment, listening to the sounds of the wilderness coming alive outside - birds chirping, a gentle breeze rustling the trees, a nearby stream babbling over rocks. She felt a thrill of excitement remembering where she was. Yosemite National Park. Hundreds of miles from her small hometown of Clarksville and the unfulfilling routine of her daily life. Out here, anything was possible.

Sitting in her sleeping bag, Jane breathed in the crisp morning air. Disheveled, she emerged from her tent to take in the view. Half Dome rose nearly 5,000 feet above her campsite. Wispy clouds clung to the dome's ridges like cotton candy. Jane grinned, wondering what adventure today would bring.

Jane efficiently broke down her campsite after a quick breakfast of oatmeal and tea. She had grown more confident in her wilderness skills after several days in Yosemite. Mark Watson, the handsome park ranger who had taken Jane under his wing, would surely be impressed by her self-sufficiency. The thought of Mark made Jane blush slightly.

She consulted her map and decided on a 12-mile hike through forests, meadows, and the Merced River. She filled her hydration pack with water from the nearby spigot and slipped on her hiking boots. Slinging her backpack over her shoulders, Jane set off down the trail away from the main campgrounds. The further she got from other hikers, the more thrilling the solitude became. Out here, it was just her and nature.

Jane hiked steadily all morning, stopping periodically to rest and refill her water bottle in crystal-clear streams. Around midday, she entered a shady pine forest, the trees soaring hundreds of feet into the sky. Jane craned her neck, awe-struck by the primeval majesty surrounding her. A comfortable silence enveloped her, interrupted only by the call of a hawk high above.

Caught in the natural splendor, Jane wandered off the main trail to explore the forest. She imagined herself an intrepid explorer of old. After about an hour of weaving between massive tree trunks, however, Jane glanced down at her compass with a start. The path disappeared, and her heart raced. She was lost.

Frantically consulting her map proved useless with a point of reference. The trees stretched endlessly in every direction, indistinguishable from one another. Jane's mouth went dry with rising panic.

The sun was setting; she had no cell service or way to find her way back. Night fell fast in the wilderness. Jane would be utterly alone, exposed to the elements and whatever creatures roamed these woods after dark.

"HELP!" Jane yelled in desperation, her voice echoing through the eerily silent forest. "CAN ANYBODY HEAR ME?"

Only the startled caw of a raven answered her cry. Jane sank on an overturned log, fighting back tears. She scolded herself for letting her overconfidence lead her astray. How could she have been so reckless? Mark had trusted her to take his survival lessons to heart. Now, she was lost in the untamed wilderness with darkness rapidly closing in.

Wrapping her arms around herself against the sudden chill, Jane strained her ears for any sound of approaching rescuers. But she was miles from the nearest trail or campsite. The likelihood of a random passerby hearing her shouts was infinitesimally small. As total darkness fell, Jane gathered pine boughs and dead leaves to make a rudimentary shelter, just as Mark had shown her. She huddled beneath it; body wracked with shivers from the cold and blind terror. Sleep was impossible. Every rustle or snap of a branch jolted Jane upright, pulse racing. She thought of her cozy home apartment with central heating and locked doors; what she wouldn't give to be safely inside its four walls!

Time crawled by at a torturous pace. After what felt like an eternity, Jane detected flashlights bobbing through the trees in the distance. "OVER HERE!" she screamed with every ounce of remaining energy. "I'M OVER HERE!" The lights turned in her direction, and blessed voices called, "Hello! Where are you!"

Jane stumbled out from beneath her shelter toward the lights, sobbing with relief. A familiar tall, broad-shouldered figure came into view, holding a flashlight aloft. Mark! Never in her life had Jane been so happy to see someone.

"Jane! Thank God, I found you," Mark said. He wrapped her in a quick, tight hug. "Are you okay? Are you hurt?" His dark eyes searched her face, creased with concern beneath the brim of his ranger hat.

Jane shook her head, still struggling to form words through her tears. "No, I'm fine," she finally choked out. "Just so scared and relieved to see you."

Mark kept an arm wrapped firmly around Jane's shoulders as he led her through the dark woods, retracing the path he had come. Two other rangers trailed behind.

"I'm so sorry," Jane said faintly, embarrassed by her carelessness. "I shouldn't have gone wandering off the trail like an idiot."

"You're not an idiot," Mark said gently. "It was a mistake, but getting lost in the woods can happen so easily to any hiker. What matters is you made a shelter and kept your wits until help arrived. You did everything right."

She had stopped trembling when they returned to Jane's campsite beneath Half Dome. One of the rangers got a fire going while Mark fetched blankets for Jane. She revived herself with hot tea and some rehydrating food packs as the color returned to her cheeks. The four sat around the crackling fire as complete darkness enveloped the camp. Jane kept glancing at Mark, sitting strong and capable across from her. He had come to her rescue like a guardian angel. There was no way she could ever properly thank him.

After the other rangers left to resume their patrol, Mark stayed by the fire with Jane. Neither was eager to turn in after the harrowing events of the night. Jane gazed into the leaping flames, comforted by their warmth and Mark's steadfast presence.

"I'm so glad you're okay," Mark said softly. "I was worried about you." He gave a self-conscious half-smile that made Jane's heart flip.

Emboldened by the intimacy of the firelit night, Jane decided to open up to Mark in a way she never had with anyone else. She told him about growing up in sleepy Creeksville, where her only adventures came from books, how she had played it safe her whole life, avoiding risks. How coming to Yosemite alone had been her first honest attempt to break out of her rut.

"I want to experience more but I'm afraid," she admitted. "I followed a simple path and now I'm going through the motions. My life is the opposite of this place - wild, free."

Mark paused before responding. "It's not too late, you know. This trip can be a fresh start. A chance to listen to your heart instead of your fears for once." He absently tossed a pinecone into the flames. "Life is out there waiting to be lived boldly. Seize the opportunity."

Jane let his words sink in, staring into the glowing embers. Mark was right. She had been granted an opportunity to reinvent herself beyond the confines of Creeksville. It was terrifying but thrilling. For the first time, Jane truly believed transformation was possible.

The next morning, Mark devoted the day to teaching Jane more wilderness survival skills. He showed her how to read the landscape for clues about direction and water sources. Together, they constructed a basic lean-to shelter from fallen logs and pine boughs. Mark demonstrated filtering murky puddle water through charcoal and sand to make it potable.

"You'd be surprised how long you can survive out here with just basic skills," he told Jane. She concentrated intently, determined to ingrain these invaluable lessons. She never again wanted to feel as helpless as she had the night before.

By late afternoon, Jane could confidently start a fire with flint and steel, pack an emergency survival bag, and identify edible berries. Her admiration for Mark deepened along with her wilderness competency.

As the sun began to set in vivid hues of orange and fuschia, Mark turned to Jane with a smile. "How about we go on a special hike tomorrow morning?" Jane's curiosity was piqued. "I'm in!" she replied eagerly. She imagined them ascending some hidden mountain trail in the mystical predawn light. It seemed intensely romantic. Mark smiled again, touching her lightly before heading off to his campsite. Jane watched him go, skin tingling where his hand had been.

The following day, at 4:30 a.m., Jane was up and ready to meet Mark in the cold darkness. She was surprised to see four other hikers had joined them on this sunrise adventure. Their headlamps bobbed like fireflies as the group made their way up a steep trail Mark was leading them on. Conversation was minimal at this early hour, but the anticipation felt electric.

An hour of climbing brought them to the summit, a rocky outcrop with panoramic views. The night sky was beginning to lighten. Mark pointed out the best spots along the ridgeline to watch the sun emerge over the ragged horizon. Jane settled herself on a flat-topped boulder, hugging her knees. Mark sat close beside her. Neither needed to speak as they waited in contemplative wonder for the dawn.

Jane caught her breath when the fiery rays crested the distant peaks, brightening almost imperceptibly and then flooding the sky with molten gold. It was the most incredible sunrise she had ever witnessed. The shifting colors rising over the alien, primeval landscape made her feel simultaneously insignificant yet connected to every living thing under the vast sky.

Jane turned to see if Mark was equally moved, only to find him gazing right at her. "Magnificent, isn't it?" he murmured. Caught in his intent stare, Jane could only nod, hoping the dim light concealed her blush.

The group lingered until the sun shone in the cloudless blue dome above. As they began the descent back to camp, Mark stepped beside Jane. "Thanks for convincing me to get up at that ungodly hour," Jane joked. "It was worth every minute."

Mark smiled. "I had a hunch you'd appreciate it. Sunrise and sunset are sacred times in nature - the chance to witness life renewing itself." He paused. "It's a privilege to share that with someone."

Jane's own life felt renewed after that magical dawn. She had come to Yosemite to discover unknown parts of herself, and the journey was beginning. With Mark as her guide and guardian, she was ready to embrace whatever came next.

Chapter 5

Jane blinked awake slowly, momentarily disoriented. It took her a few seconds to remember where she was - not in her queen bed back home in San Francisco but tucked under a scratchy wool blanket on a lumpy couch in the middle of the Sierras. Early morning light filtered through the dusty cabin windows, illuminating the sparse room.

With a groan, Jane sat up and gingerly rotated her ankle, grimacing at the swelling. Her fall yesterday was worse than she thought. She didn't know what she would've done without Chris finding her stranded and helpless on the trail.

Speaking of Chris, Jane could hear him rattling around the small kitchen area, humming under his breath. She felt a nervous flutter in her stomach remembering their cozy dinner last night, how he gently bandaged her ankle, his strong hands lightly grasping her calf. The way his blue eyes crinkled at the edges when he laughed at her stories about disastrous hiking mishaps. She tried to ignore the spark she felt. It was too soon after her breakup with Mike for anything like that. Chris was probably being a good Samaritan.

Still, she couldn't deny the thrill of Chris appearing and holding two steaming mugs. "Morning! I made coffee. I wasn't sure if you took cream and sugar, so I brought some over."

He set the mugs on the coffee table and offered Jane a crooked smile. Jane's breath hitched looking into his tanned, rugged face and kind eyes. Get it together! she scolded herself. Don't make this weird.

"Thanks, I take it black," Jane said, hoping her flushed cheeks weren't noticeable. She took a sip, savoring the smoky bitterness.

Chris settled into an old leather armchair with his mug. "So, how's the ankle feeling today?"

Jane rotated it again and winced. "Still pretty sore and swollen. But I think the wrap you put on it really helped. I appreciate you taking care of me."

Chris waved her off. "Don't mention it. Couldn't let you hobble all the way back down in the state you were in. What happened out there anyway? That stretch along Vernal Falls can be tricky if you're not paying attention."

Jane looked down, cheeks flaming in embarrassment. "Ugh, honestly I feel so dumb. I was daydreaming about something stupid and didn't watch my footing. Stepped right onto a wet rock and went down hard. I'm usually more alert than that on the trail."

"Hey, don't beat yourself up," Chris said kindly. "It could've happened to anyone. I've just seen a lot of nasty slips on that granite when people aren't focused. Main thing is you're safe now."

His reassurance made Jane feel a bit better. They sat chatting comfortably about Yosemite and swapping funny stories from the trail. Chris had been a ranger here for nearly ten years, and his deep love and knowledge of the park was evident. Jane was captivated by listening to him gush about secret waterfalls and the ancient giant sequoias that amazed him no matter how often he saw them. She could picture them hiking together, Chris pointing out hidden wonders. A pang of longing caught her off guard.

"How about some breakfast?" Chris asked, breaking her reverie. "I've got eggs, pancake mix..."

"Pancakes sound amazing," Jane said. She started to get up, but Chris waved her back down.

"You just relax that ankle. Cooking is the least I can do."

Jane smiled, settling back against the threadbare cushions. She watched Chris bustle around the kitchen, admiring the flex of his forearms as he mixed up batter. Jane had to stifle a grin when he appeared, balancing two plates loaded with fluffy golden pancakes. Spraining her ankle had some perks, after all.

Over breakfast, they got to know each other better, chatting about their lives outside these Sierra granite walls. Chris was 35, just a few years older than Jane's 29. He was born in Oregon and moved around with his forest ranger dad's postings before settling in Yosemite. The stories flowed so quickly it felt like talking to an old friend, their laughter coming quickly and often. Jane could almost forget the gnawing heartbreak of her recent breakup that sent her desperately fleeing here alone.

When their plates were clean, Chris insisted on re-wrapping Jane's injury. She perched on the couch and carefully peeled off the tensor bandage, wincing as her puffy, bruised ankle was revealed. Chris maintained a professional detachment as he gently manipulated it, checking the swelling. However, Jane still felt hyper-aware of his fingers grazing her bare skin. She made small talk to distract herself from the tingles shooting up her leg.

"This place is incredible," Jane said, gazing around the cozy cabin. "Have you really lived here for 10 years?"

Chris nodded, smoothing a fresh wrap around her arch. "Yeah, since my divorce I wanted a remote spot away from everything to kind of reset. The park rents this cabin out to employees."

Jane's ears perked up at this personal detail, but she kept her voice casual. "Divorce must've been really hard. I actually just got out of a 5-year relationship, so I can relate."

Chris paused, thumb lightly grazing her heel. "It wasn't an easy time, that's for sure. My ex-wife and I got married young, right out of college. Thought it would last forever." He gave a rueful little laugh. "Anyway, it's been 3 years now. Ancient history."

Jane's breath caught as his eyes met hers. An unspoken understanding passed between them. The cozy cabin suddenly felt several degrees warmer.

Chris cleared his throat, turning back to wrap her ankle. "All set. I don't think it's broken, just a bad sprain. I'd stay off it as much as possible for a few days."

"Yes, doctor," Jane teased. The joking tone eased the tension. She wasn't imagining things, was she? The spark of interest when their eyes met, the way Chris lingered close after finishing the wrap? Jane looked away, confused and embarrassed by her traitorous thoughts.

They spent the next couple of days in casual companionship. Jane took it easy on the couch, reading and journaling, her ankle propped up on a pillow. Chris came by on breaks from his patrols to check on her, bringing dinner or playing card games. In the evenings, they sat sipping bourbon (Jane insisted she didn't have a disability) and talking until the stars burned bright through the windows. Their conversation flowed easily from childhood memories to future dreams, skirting around but never directly acknowledging the tension.

With each day, Jane's ankle improved, though she found reasons to linger. She knew she should continue her trip soon. Still, the thought of leaving the cozy cabin - and Chris' company - made her unaccountably sad. She tried to ignore the pang in her chest when he left for work in the mornings. This was ridiculous. They hardly knew each other, and Jane refused to be that girl caught up in a rebound fling. Even if the thought of Chris' stubble rough against her cheek, his warm hands framing her hips made her dizzy. Nope, she was not going there.

On the fourth evening, Jane sat curled on the couch beneath a quilt reading. She was immersed in the pages, nearly forgetting the empty cabin around her, when the sound of Chris' truck on the gravel driveway jolted her back. She felt suddenly self-conscious in her oversized sleep shirt and messy topknot.

Chris appeared in the doorway holding a brown paper bag. "Brought dinner from the village," he said with an easy smile that weakened Jane's knees. "Hope you like tacos."

They worked in the small kitchen, Jane chopping onions and tomatoes as Chris grilled meat on the stove. He squeezed lime over the sizzling beef, sending up a mouth-watering aroma. Jane's heart swelled at how naturally they operated together in this domestic scene, chatting and joking as they cooked. She could get used to this.

Soon, they were sitting across from each other, plates loaded with tacos and beers at hand. Chris told a silly story about finding a blaze-orange fanny pack forgotten deep in the backcountry, and Jane laughed so hard she nearly choked on her carnitas. Their knees accidentally brushed under the table, and Jane felt her cheeks flush. She scolded herself to get it together.

After dinner, Chris stoked a fire in the stone fireplace while Jane made hot toddies, the whiskey steaming as she poured. They settled onto the couch with their mugs closer than usual. Heat radiated from Chris' thigh mere inches from Jane's tucked legs. She sipped her drink slowly to calm her nerves.

"Thanks for dinner," Jane said, looking into his eyes. The firelight danced there.

"Of course," he said. "It's been great having your company this week. Livened up my solo bachelor lifestyle." His tone was light, but his gaze was intense.

Jane's chest constricted. "It's been so good getting to know you," she said softly. Unthinking, she reached her hand to graze his where it rested on his thigh. Chris froze at her touch but didn't pull away.

They sat suspended in the moment, the crackling fire filling the silence. Ever so slowly, Chris lifted his hand to cup Jane's cheek, rough thumb tracing the rise of her cheekbone. Jane's breath caught, the rest of the world falling away. Unable to stop herself, Jane turned her face into his touch, nuzzling against his warm palm.

Chris' eyes darkened, his grip on her cheek tightening. He slid his other hand around Jane's waist and smoothly pulled her against his chest. Her heart hammered as his stubbled jaw grazed her forehead her temple.

"Jane," he whispered into her hair, his breath hot on her cheek. That was all it took. Jane lifted her face to his, and their lips collided, pent-up longing breaking loose like a dam inside her. She dissolved against him, hands gripping his muscular shoulders as the kiss deepened urgently. Chris' arms locked around her, crushing her supple curves into his hard planes.

It could have been minutes or hours later when they finally broke apart, hearts pounding in rhythm. Chris gazed down at Jane, his eyes wide with wonder as he saw her clearly for the first time. Jane's whole body hummed. She took his hand without a word and led him to the small bedroom in the back of the cabin.

Moonlight streamed through the wooden-framed windows as they stood at the foot of the bed, a tangle of wandering hands and fervent kisses. Piece by piece, their clothing fell away until skin met in exquisite sensation. Chris lowered Jane reverently onto the quilt, and she welcomed him into her, wanting nothing between them anymore.

Jane awoke slowly the following day, momentarily confused by the warm body curled around her, unfamiliar sheets tangled around their legs. Then it came flooding back in a rush - the fire, the kiss, fumbling laughingly into bed together, the hours after when their bodies communicated all the words left unsaid. She flushed, remembering the sounds Chris drew from her that she didn't know she could make.

Propped up on one elbow, Jane allowed herself to look at him. Chris' face was smoothed of its usual careworn expression, hair charmingly disheveled. He looked so much younger asleep. Jane's heart constricted. Was it crazy that she already imagined this face across from her every morning? She quashed the thought. Some rebound fling this was turning into.

Chris opened his eyes and smiled sleepily. "Morning," he murmured, tucking a strand of hair behind her ear. The tender gesture sent Jane's mind spinning years down the road. Lazy Sundays in bed together, cozy holidays nestled before the fire, steamy nights between these sheets. It was too perfect, to be honest.

After lingering in bed exchanging soft, unhurried kisses, they finally rose to make breakfast. Chris whipped up cheese omelets, and Jane sliced grapefruit, each finding excuses to brush up against the other. Their conversation flowed easily around mundane topics like the weather, but an undercurrent hummed below the surface. Jane felt giddy in a way she hadn't since her early days with Mike. Could this be happening so soon after her world shattered? She tamped down the hope rising in her chest.

Over breakfast dishes, Jane ventured cautiously, "I can probably try hiking out tomorrow if my ankle's up for it..." She trailed off, peeking sideways to gauge Chris' reaction.

He paused, shoulders tensing almost imperceptibly. "Right, of course. You've got your whole trip ahead of you still."

Jane's stomach clenched at his neutral tone. Was he trying to distance himself subtly? She backpedaled. My itinerary is flexible. I can stick around here a bit longer if..."

Chris busied himself scrubbing the cast iron pan, his jaw tight. Dread crept up Jane's throat. Was she reading this all wrong?

"Listen, Jane..." Chris began, then stopped, searching for words. He turned off the water and faced her. "Last night was really amazing. But I need to be upfront. I'm just not in a place for anything serious with you, or anyone, right now."

Jane looked down, cheeks flaming in embarrassment. So it was just a hookup for him. She was an idiot to think otherwise.

Oblivious to her spiraling thoughts, Chris went on, "I'm so sorry if I led you on. You're incredible, truly. But after my divorce I promised myself I'd stay solo and focus on my work. I hope we can still be friends?"

Jane forced a smile that felt more like a grimace. Friends who occasionally hook up when it's convenient for him? She needed out of there.

"Hey, no need to apologize," she managed lightly, hoping the mortification burning through her wasn't obvious. "You've been really kind letting me stay here. And don't worry about my ankle, I'm sure I can make it home fine tomorrow if I take it slow."

Chris looked relieved, which stung more than Jane cared to admit. She mumbled an excuse about packing her stuff and escaped to the bedroom before the stinging in her eyes spilled over. Sinking onto the edge of the bed, Jane dropped her head into her hands and took a shuddering breath. God, she was so stupid. Of course, he just saw her as a distraction, some fun company for a few days. At least Mike had loved her once. Chris never cared at all.

The rest of the day dragged by awkwardly. Jane puttered around slowly, repacking her gear while Chris was on patrol. When he returned in the evening, they danced uncomfortably around each other in the kitchen, and their easy rapport vanished. Jane escaped outside after forcing down some soup, needing space to clear her head.

She limped to the edge of the woods bordering the back of the cabin and sat gingerly on a fallen log, wincing as pain radiated up her leg. The fresh mountain air helped calm her whirling thoughts. Looking up at the ancient pines silhouetted against the dusky pink sky, the past week's events felt strangely distant. In days, she had nearly forgotten why she fled here in the first place - to mend her shattered heart. Instead, she let herself be momentarily dazzled by the danger of something new and thrilling. And look where that got her.

Jane hung her head, ashamed of her neediness and stupidity. Her priority needed to be taking care of herself, not rushing into the arms of any man who showed her kindness and adventure. She resolved to continue her trip first thing in the morning. Chris was right - they barely knew each other. It was foolish even to entertain ideas of anything real developing between them.

Jane rose gingerly. The sun had slipped below the jagged horizon, and her ankle throbbed. She steeled herself to go inside and awkwardly get through this last night. She could be on the road tomorrow, putting physical and emotional distance between her and Chris. She just had to keep her chin up a little longer.

Jane limped back into an empty living room. Chris was clattering in the kitchen. Thankful for a moment alone, she lowered herself onto the lumpy couch. Running a hand over her face, Jane let out a long breath. These past days felt like an emotional rollercoaster ending in an embarrassing crash she wanted only to forget. At least soon, she could start fresh elsewhere.

Chris appeared holding two chipped mugs and a sheepish expression. "Thought some tea could help. Sleepytime okay?"

"Sure, thanks," Jane murmured, taking the mug he offered. The scent of chamomile wafted up, and despite herself, she instantly felt soothed. They sat sipping the steaming tea in silence until Chris spoke again softly.

"Hey, I need to apologize about earlier. I didn't mean to be insensitive about...us." He cleared his throat, struggling uncharacteristically for words. "I know I'm not great at talking about feelings and stuff. But I meant what I said about you being incredible. These few days getting to know you have really meant a lot."

He looked at Jane with such earnestness she felt her defensiveness cracking. This was still the same kind, thoughtful man who came to her rescue and cared for her for days without a second thought. She managed a small smile.

"I appreciate you saying that. And I get it - I'm clearly working through my own stuff too. It was unrealistic to put expectations on this...whatever this was." Jane exhaled, feeling some of the day's tension leave her body. "Let's just call it an adventure and leave it at that."

Chris smiled back, the easy warmth returning between them. "I'd toast to that." He lifted his mug. Jane clinked it with her own, the ceramic chiming sweetly. She settled back into the couch cushions, a pleasant, sleepy calm settling in.

Maybe they didn't know what the next day would bring once she hit the road again alone. But right now, Jane was content to share this quiet moment.

Chapter 6

Jane slowly turned her sedan into the familiar driveway of her apartment complex, gravel crunching under the tires. She had driven straight through from New Mexico, exhaustion and sadness pressing on her shoulders. Pulling into her assigned parking spot, Jane rested her forehead on the steering wheel and exhaled.

Home. She was home after her disastrous solo camping trip that impulsive adventure meant to add color to her mundane life. Instead, she felt more lost than ever.

With a heavy sigh, Jane hauled herself out of the car. The late summer air was thick and humid, without the crisp pine scent of the mountains. She popped the trunk and lugged her camping gear upstairs. Inside her modest apartment, she let the bags slump to the floor.

Jane's eyes prickled with hot tears as she looked around. Nothing had changed; not one thing in the weeks she had been gone. Yet she felt like a different person now. A fool who had risked everything to chase a fantasy had a broken heart.

Wiping her eyes, Jane noticed the flashing light on her answering machine. She pressed play, and Amy's bubbly voice filled the somber space.

"Jane! It's Amy. Just checking to see if you're back from your trip yet. Call me as soon as you get this, I'm dying to hear all about your wilderness adventures! Hope you had an amazing time. Oh, and welcome home!"

Jane managed a small smile. Dear sweet Amy, I am enthusiastic about Jane's ill-fated journey into the unknown. With a lump in her throat, Jane deleted the message. She couldn't bear to tell Amy about John, the handsome forest ranger who had opened her eyes to nature's beauty yet crushed her fragile hopes of love.

Too exhausted to unpack or eat, Jane stumbled to her bedroom. Kicking off her hiking boots, she collapsed onto the mattress. Mars, her ginger tabby cat, trotted over and curled beside her. His familiar rumbling purr soothed Jane's aching heart as she drifted asleep.

Morning came too quickly, sunlight streaming through the cheap vinyl blinds. Jane groaned and pulled a pillow over her head. She had almost forgotten it was Monday. The first day of the teacher workweek before students arrived.

Reluctantly, Jane got out of bed and shuffled to the bathroom, avoiding the mirror. She already knew her eyes were swollen from crying herself to sleep. Turning the shower handle to hot, Jane stepped under the scalding spray as if she could wash away the heartbreak and shame from her trip.

After scrubbing every inch of her body, Jane toweled off and tucked her damp hair into a loose bun. Standing in front of her closet, she wondered what to wear to work after her torrid affair with a forest ranger.

Jane pulled on a simple navy pencil skirt and pale blue blouse. Conservative, professional, and utterly dull. Slipping her feet into a pair of beige ballet flats, Jane deemed her outfit presentable. As ready as she'd ever be to face her colleagues after the most extended break of her career.

Before leaving, Jane filled Mars's food bowl and gave him an apologetic pat. "See you tonight, bud."

The twenty-minute drive to Cherrywood Elementary passed in a blur. Jane gripped the steering wheel tightly, her knuckles white. She wasn't sure if she was ready to return to the cheerful halls of the school that had always felt like home. Not when she felt so conflicted inside.

Turning into the parking lot, Jane took a deep breath. You can do this, she told herself as she cut the engine—time to get back to reality.

Pushing through the heavy double doors, Jane let the familiar sights and smells envelope her. Brightly colored paper cut-outs decorated the front office, the lingering scent of disinfectant from the thorough summer cleaning. She made her way to her classroom, chest tight with nerves.

But as Jane stepped across the threshold into the cozy space, she felt herself relax. Everything was just as she had left it in June. Her desk was neatly organized with a potted succulent plant she had nurtured for years. The square tables the reading nook with oversized beanbag chairs and plush rug, were spaced evenly apart.

Jane ran a hand over the smooth laminate countertops as she made her way to her desk. She was back in the place that had been her haven for the past seven years. Creeksville may not have majestic forests and windswept peaks, but it has continuity. Roots.

At that moment, a cheerful voice called out from the doorway. "Jane! It's so good to see you."

Jane saw Sandy, her teaching assistant, smiling as she approached. Sandy's enthusiasm was infectious, and Jane felt the corners of her mouth turn up.

"Sandy, hi! It's wonderful to see you too," Jane replied warmly. Though her trip had ended disastrously, it felt comforting to be surrounded by familiar faces again.

"How was your summer?" Sandy asked. "Did you travel anywhere exciting?"

Jane hesitated. "Oh, you know, it was relaxing," she said vaguely. She wasn't ready to reveal the true nature of her trip to anyone yet, least of all cheerful, uncomplicated Sandy. "How about you?" she asked, deflecting.

Jane tidied the classroom as Sandy launched into a detailed account of her summer lounging by various local swimming holes. She wasn't ready to fully engage in conversation yet, needing time to process her swirling emotions.

Mercifully, the first morning meeting on the year's curriculum began on time. Jane sat in the back of the stuffy multipurpose room, half listening to the principal's enthusiastic speech about educational goals and community partnership. Mostly, she just sipped burnt coffee and doodled aimlessly in her notebook.

During a break between speakers, Mark Bennett slid into the seat beside Jane. Mark was a fellow elementary teacher, divorced with two teenagers. Though polite acquaintances, Jane wouldn't say she knew Mark well. He taught fourth grade, whereas she taught kindergarten. Their paths crossed only occasionally in the parking lot or teachers' lounge. But it was nice to see a friendly face.

"Hey Jane. Good summer?" Mark asked casually. But his warm brown eyes showed genuine interest.

"Oh yes, it was...relaxing," Jane said, recycling the same noncommittal response she had given Sandy.

Mark smiled, the corners of his eyes crinkling. "You'll have to tell me about it sometime."

Before Jane could respond, the principal had resumed droning on about assessment goals and curriculum integration. But Mark's invitation lingered in Jane's mind. Did he want to get to know her better? The thought was surprising yet appealing. Mark had always been kind, and he was rather handsome now that Jane took the time to notice...

The day passed in a blur of administrative paperwork and classroom organizing. When the dismissal bell rang at 3 p.m., Jane felt drained. She returned home to another flashing message from Amy about meeting up for cocktails soon. With a twinge of guilt, Jane deleted it once again.

Collapsing onto the lumpy futon, Jane reached for her paperback copy of Where the Crawdads Sing. But even her favorite lyrical novel couldn't hold her interest tonight. With a huff, she tossed the book aside. Mars hopped into her lap, purring contentedly as Jane stroked his soft fur.

"Why can't I stop thinking about him, Mars?" Jane sighed into the quiet apartment. John's rugged face and muscular arms kept invading her thoughts, as much as she tried to block the memories. His green eyes sparked with adventure as he led her on risky mountain hikes to scenic vistas—the feeling of his calloused hand covering hers as he helped her start a campfire.

Jane squeezed her eyes shut, shaking her head sharply. It was no use dwelling on what would never be. John had made it crystal clear he didn't want any commitment with her or anyone.

"I was a fool to think otherwise," Jane whispered bitterly. With a broken spirit, she drifted off to sleep; Mars curled beside her.

The first two weeks of September passed in a blur of meet-the-teacher nights, lesson-planning sessions, and curriculum meetings. Jane fell into the familiar rhythms of the school year, appreciating the busyness that left her little time to dwell on the past.

When her students arrived after Labor Day, their exuberant energy and joyful smiles filled Jane with renewed purpose. Their sweet faces looked at her with such trust, seeing her as their guide in this new phase of their lives. Jane couldn't help but feel pride that these children were under her care. She would nurture their growth as diligently as she tended the plants in her classroom garden. Their innocence was a balm to her bruised spirit.

On Friday afternoon, Jane lingered in her classroom after the students left, tidying up art supplies and wiping down tables. She still hadn't spoken to Amy since returning from the trip, and their usual Friday happy hour tradition felt like a lifetime ago. Sinking into the chair at her desk, Jane knew she couldn't avoid her friend forever. She would call Amy this weekend and tell her a watered-down version of the truth. Amy deserved that much.

A soft rap at the open door jolted Jane from her thoughts. She glanced up to see Mark leaning against the doorframe, looking unfairly attractive in a simple blue button-down that matched his eyes.

Mark asked if I wanted to grab dinner with him tonight. He gave her a crooked, hopeful smile.

Jane blinked in surprise. Was Mark Bennett asking her on a date? They had only exchanged casual small talk over stale coffee in the lounge.

Jane had never noticed him as anything more than a colleague. But the way he gazed at her with such tenderness suggested deeper feelings she had been oblivious to.

"Oh, um, sure. I'd love to," Jane stammered out, a blush rising to her cheeks. Mark's whole face lit up at her acceptance, and Jane felt an unexpected rush of pleasure. She had forgotten what it was like to be looked at with such genuine care and interest. It was a heady feeling after the detached coldness of John.

"Great!" Mark said. "How does six o'clock sound? There's a great little Italian place I've been wanting to try."

They exchanged numbers finalized details, and Mark practically bounced out of her classroom. As Jane gathered her things to leave for the weekend, she marveled at this sudden turn of events. Less than a month ago, she cried over a failed affair. A romantic date with a man she had overlooked for years. What a difference a day makes.

Scrubbing off a week's dry-erase marker stains in the shower, Jane pondered what to wear for this unexpected date. Mark had only ever seen her in modest blouses and sensible slacks suitable for chasing after five-year-olds. She wanted to make an effort tonight.

After debating for far too long, Jane selected a flattering wrap dress in a vibrant cobalt blue. The color set off her chestnut hair and hazel eyes. She curled her hair and swiped on a hint of mascara. Checking her reflection, she let out a relieved breath. The woman staring back at her with a hint of a smile looked poised and lovely, not heartbroken and adrift. It was a start.

Promptly at six, Mark pulled up outside her apartment building. Jane felt unaccountably shy as she slid into his sedan with a timid hello. But Mark's enthusiasm instantly put her at ease.

"Jane! You look beautiful," he said sincerely. A light flush spread across Jane's cheeks at the compliment.

During the short drive, they chatted about their students and classes. Jane found herself appreciating Mark's compassion and dedication as a teacher. He spoke about his eighth graders with such care and understanding.

Mark held the door for Jane at the restaurant, guiding her inside with a light touch at the small of her back. The considerate gesture brought a smile to her face. He was a gentleman, so different from the emotionally remote John.

Over spinach salads and chicken parmesan, their conversation flowed easily. Mark made Jane laugh with amusing stories of field trips gone awry. His steady brown gaze and attentive questions soon had her opening up about her classroom hopes and struggles. She even told him about her ill-fated trip, glossing over any mention of John. It just felt so natural to talk to Mark. Comfortable in a way she hadn't experienced with someone in a very long time.

After dinner, Mark took Jane's hand. "I meant it when I said I want to get to know you better." "You're an incredible woman, Jane."

Jane's pulse quickened at his earnest words. She turned her hand palm up to link her fingers through his. The touch was warm and grounding. Looking into Mark's tender eyes, she felt ready to take a chance.

"I'd like that," Jane said softly. And she meant it. Mark's solid presence made her feel safe in a way she hadn't known she needed. Maybe her world could still have traces of magic, even far from mist-shrouded mountains.

They walked back to her apartment hand in hand, footsteps ideally in sync. Mark drew Jane close outside the entryway and kissed her with aching sweetness. She melted into him, letting the kiss wash away the last bitter remnants of her heartbreak.

When Mark finally pulled back, Jane smiled brighter than she had in months. He whispered goodnight and squeezed her hand before heading to his car. Jane watched him go, her heart full of hope.

That weekend, Jane finally mustered the courage to call Amy. Curled on the sofa with a fresh cup of tea, she selected Amy's name from her contacts and hit dial before she could overthink it.

After a few rings, Amy's bubbly voice answered. "Jane! Oh my gosh, it is so good to hear your voice. I've missed you!"

Instantly, tears pricked Jane's eyes. She had missed her best friend terribly. "Hi, Amy. I'm so sorry I didn't call sooner. I just needed time to process everything after I returned," she said honestly.

"Don't apologize, I totally understand. Just start from the beginning and tell me everything!"

So Jane did, giving Amy a truncated yet truthful account of her trip. The stunning vistas and treacherous hikes. Meeting John and feeling an instant connection. He pulled away emotionally at the end, leaving her confused and hurt.

Amy listened sympathetically, only interjecting an occasional soft gasp or murmur. When Jane finally finished, she let out a long breath. It felt cathartic to confess it all out loud.

"Oh, sweetie, I'm so sorry," Amy said gently. "What a rollercoaster. But honestly? It sounds like John was totally wrong for you. You deserve someone who is as brave and loyal and passionate as you are."

Jane smiled, wiping away a stray tear. "Thanks, Amy. That means a lot to hear." She went on to tell Amy about her date with Mark the night before. How comfortable and safe she felt with him. He looked at her like she held the universe's secrets in her eyes.

"Oooh, Jane. He sounds wonderful!" Amy exclaimed. "I told you there are great guys right in our little town. When do I get to meet him?"

They spent the next hour chatting about getting drinks together with Mark shortly. Jane felt lighter than she had weeks after opening up to her closest friend. She knew Amy would help stitch the frayed pieces of her spirit back together.

Over the next few weeks, Jane settled into a comfortable routine. Mornings were filled with crafts, singing circle times, and recess playdates. Evenings were often spent curled up on the sofa with Mark, laughing over takeout containers as they swapped stories about their day. And weekends brought Saturday morning brunch dates with Amy to their favorite corner café.

Jane no longer thought about running off to distant lands for adventure. She was starting to realize that life's true magic was often right in front of her, in quiet moments passing all too quickly. The magic was in her students' unrestrained laughter on the playground. Her cat was dozing blissfully in a patch of sunlight—Mark's strong hand enveloping hers as they took a stroll around the neighborhood.

The brilliant New Mexico sunsets now faded to a distant memory. Jane was learning to appreciate the simple joys Creeksville offered. And maybe she had finally found someone willing to explore those joys by her side.

Chapter 7

Jane awoke feeling refreshed and rejuvenated Friday morning after a restful night's sleep. Sunlight streamed in as she stretched, content after a long week of teaching. She felt energized and excited for the day ahead.

Jane had coffee and breakfast, then hurried to school. She chose a cheerful yellow blouse and a flowing floral skirt, wanting to match the brightness of the sunny spring day. As she styled her hair into a side braid, Jane thought about the creative new lesson plans she had developed, inspired by her rejuvenating weekend trip to the botanical gardens. She couldn't wait to see her students' reactions.

Jane arrived at Washington Elementary with a skip in her step. She breezed through the halls, exchanging chipper hellos with fellow teachers. Settling in at her desk, Jane neatly arranged the supplies for today's creative writing session—stacks of construction paper in a rainbow of colors, markers, crayons, and glitter glue. She had also printed out unique writing prompts inspired by the plants and scenery from the gardens.

At the ring of the first bell, students started filtering into the classroom. Jane warmly greeted each one by name, admiring the bright shirts and flower hair clips so many girls had worn to match the springtime spirit of the day. Once all 25 students had arrived, Jane quieted the chatter and announced they would start the day with a creative writing project.

"Today we're going to let our imaginations bloom just like the flowers and trees outside," Jane began, holding up a vibrant pink sheet of paper. "You can choose any color paper and use the writing prompts I've put out to craft a nature-inspired story, poem or scene. Feel free to illustrate your writing as well. Be as creative as you'd like!"

The students were instantly abuzz with excitement. Jane passed out paper and art supplies as the kids debated prompts and colors. Soon, the room was filled with pencils scratching, markers squeaking, and the occasional giggle or gasp of inspiration strikes. Jane circulated through the busy hum, admiring her students' creations and offering encouraging feedback. She saw imaginative tales of exploring enchanted forests, odes to the beauty of sunflowers, and adventures about befriending woodland creatures. Their enthusiasm and engagement filled her heart with joy.

The lunch bell rang all too soon, jolting Jane from the creative bubble of the classroom. She collected the students' papers, each unique and creative. "These are absolutely wonderful, everyone! I can't wait to display them in our classroom."

The kids chatted animatedly as they lined up for lunch, thrilled with the fun writing exercise. Jane stopped by the teacher's lounge on the way to the cafeteria. Her friend Kelly was already there, munching on a salad.

"Hey! How's your day going so far?" Kelly asked.

"So great!" Jane gushed as she grabbed her meal from the fridge. She described that morning's writing session in detail, from the colorful paper to the imaginative stories her students had crafted.

Kelly smiled, eyes crinkling with delight. "That sounds amazing! I'm so glad to see you excited about teaching again."

"Me too," Jane said with a contented sigh. "That trip was just what I needed to reinvigorate my creativity."

The two teachers chatted happily throughout the rest of their break. When the bell rang again, they said their goodbyes. Jane headed enthusiastically back to her classroom, replaying the morning's success over in her mind. She was filled with anticipation for that afternoon's scavenger hunt lesson.

The last school bell of the day rang at 3 p.m. sharp. Jane gathered her giddy students on the grassy field behind the school that bordered a small woodland area. She passed out magnifying glasses from a big basket.

"For today's science lesson, we're going on a nature scavenger hunt!" Jane announced. "I've made a list of things for you to look for, like interesting leaves, feathers, rocks, and more. See what treasures you can find!"

The class dispersed, scanning the landscape through their magnifiers and exclaiming over their discoveries. Jane supervised with a contented smile. She saw students cluster around a bird's nest to inspect the twigs while others examined the intricate veins of colorful leaves. Their inquisitive energy was catching.

After thirty minutes of exploration, Jane called the group back together. The kids displayed their findings excitedly.

"Look at all these amazing things we discovered just outside our school," Jane said, gesturing to the assemblage of feathers, flowers, seeds, and stones. "There's beauty and wonder all around us if we take the time to notice."

The school busses soon pulled up, and the students scampered off, still chattering about their scavenger discoveries. Jane returned inside, reflecting on the thrill of stoking her students' curiosity. She was still smiling as she tidied up her classroom before heading home.

That evening, Jane arrived early at Da Vinci's, an upscale new Italian restaurant downtown. Her friend Mark had recommended it, and they had plans to meet for dinner. The waiter showed Jane to a small table by the window. Sipping a glass of fruity pinot grigio, Jane looked over the menu of traditional pasta dishes and wood-fired pizzas.

She glanced up with a smile as Mark walked in right on time. He looked handsome in a sports coat over a button-down.

"Sorry I'm late, traffic was a mess," Mark said apologetically as he settled into his seat.

"No worries, I just sat down," Jane replied. Mark ordered a glass of Chianti, and they clinked their wine glasses together.

Their conversation flowed easily over the candlelit table as they caught up on each other's week. Jane told Mark about the school's upcoming spring concert she was helping organize. Mark made her laugh, describing the antics of the new puppy he had adopted.

When their meals arrived, Jane twirled a forkful of linguine, savoring the savory pesto sauce. Mark cut into his wood-fired pizza topped with prosciutto and arugula. They continued to chat comfortably about books, movies, and summer vacation plans.

Jane realized she was enjoying Mark's witty banter and thoughtful insights. Beneath his occasionally sarcastic exterior, he was pretty sensitive and intelligent. She felt strangely drawn to him in a way she hadn't expected. The spark between them was undeniable.

After finishing their meals, Mark invited Jane for a nightcap. Jane felt a flutter of nerves but excitement. She had always seen Mark as a friend but felt eager to explore this new connection. Jane nodded shyly in agreement.

Back at Mark's modern high-rise apartment, he poured each a glass of smooth merlot. They settled together on the leather couch; bodies angled toward each other. Mark told Jane about his recent Appalachian hiking trip as she sipped her wine. His green eyes were animated behind his glasses as he described the stunning vistas and challenging terrain.

"It sounds like an amazing trip," Jane said. She met Mark's gaze. The air between them seemed to crackle with electricity. Ever so slowly, Mark leaned in and gently pressed his lips to hers. Jane closed her eyes and kissed him back, slowly at first, then more passionately. He caressed her neck gently as she sank her fingers into his soft curls.

When they finally broke apart, flushed and breathless, Mark said softly, "Wow. I've wanted to do that for a long time."

Jane's heart pounded wildly. "Really?"

Mark nodded, looking suddenly bashful. "You're an incredible woman, Jane. Beautiful, kind, creative..." His fingers brushed her cheek. "I know this is unexpected, but I'd love to see where this leads."

Jane's head spun giddily. She was surprised and excited. "I'd love that," she said, leaning in for another kiss.

The next morning, pale sunlight filtering through the curtains woke Jane. For a moment, she was disoriented by the unfamiliar surroundings. Then she saw Mark sleeping soundly beside her, memories of last night flooding back. Jane grinned. Mark smiled back, still half asleep. "Good morning, beautiful," he murmured, pulling Jane close. She sighed happily, snuggling into his warm chest. They traded slow, sleepy kisses.

"Would you like to stay for breakfast?" Mark asked, sitting up and stretching.

"I'd love to," Jane replied. Mark loaned her an oversized t-shirt, and they headed to the sleek kitchen hand in hand. Jane leaned against the counter, watching Mark whisk eggs and scoop them into a pan to scramble. He popped bread into the toaster and poured two mugs of coffee.

Soon, they sat together at the small dining table covered in plated and steaming mugs. The eggs were fluffy and delicious. Their conversation carried the ease and intimacy of a couple who had been together far longer than a few hours. Jane's heart swelled, thinking about exploring this new relationship. The adventure had only just begun.

After breakfast, Jane headed home to change before school. All morning, she wore a permanent grin, replaying the electrifying moments with Mark. She couldn't focus on anything else. The final school bell on Friday afternoon was music to Jane's ears. She wished her students a wonderful weekend, then hurried to her car, eager for whatever fun the evening held.

As Jane drove home, sunshine warming her shoulders, she marveled at the past week's adventures. The surge of creativity followed her rejuvenating trip to the gardens it had sparked. Her authentic connection with Mark is so unexpected yet utterly right. And her students, whose bright smiles and engaged minds filled her with purpose.

Jane knew there would still be challenges ahead in her career and blossoming relationship. But she felt centered by the grounding forces of nature, creativity, and human connection - simple yet profound joys she had found in the adventure of everyday living. With an open heart and courage to explore, Jane was ready to embrace whatever life had in store next.

Don't miss out!

Visit the website below and you can sign up to receive emails whenever P E Murdock publishes a new book. There's no charge and no obligation.

https://books2read.com/r/B-A-WHGZ-HIRPC

BOOKS 2 READ

Connecting independent readers to independent writers.

About the Author

Born on January 28, 1961, Paul Ernest Murdock discovered his love for writing later in life. With a career in warehousing and an academic background in Accounting, his real-world experiences add a gritty realism to his favorite genres, crime mysteries, and thrillers. Paul's work is a thrilling blend of suspenseful plots and complex characters. When not writing, he enjoys the tranquility of outdoor activities such as bowling, camping, and fishing. Despite his late start, Paul's passion and dedication to writing demonstrate that it's never too late to pursue your passion.